MIRROR WORLD

by Keith West

Illustrated by Harriet Buckley

CHARACTERS

Jimmy Bird	a farmer's son, very timid
Daniel Waterhouse	Jimmy's adventurous friend
Mum, Daphne Bird	Jimmy's mother
Dad, Robert Bird	Jimmy's father, a farmer
Gareth Endersby	a bully
Rigby	an untrustworthy officer
Storm trooper 1 **Storm trooper 2**	} work for the Nazis
Ticket Inspector	
Herman **Bernard**	} freedom fighters
Jessica	Jewish refugee
Hannah	Jessica's sister, freedom fighter
George	elderly freedom fighter
Slug 1	
Slug 2	
Grandad, **Denis Chapman**	Jimmy's grandfather, an eccentric inventor

For Charles and Anne Rigg, who appreciate the creative writing process.

MIRROR WORLD

ACT ONE
SCENE ONE

The Bird lounge early in the morning.

DAD: What are you going to do with your day off, Jimmy? Any homework? Perhaps you'd like to help me on the farm?

JIMMY: No Dad … I … er…I –

(A cow moos in the distance)

DAD: The cows need milking. And the cabbages need attention. But you don't like picking caterpillars off cabbages, do you? You wanted the organic farm, yet you won't lift a finger to help me.

MUM: Oh, leave the boy alone, Bob. How many I.N.S.E.T. days does the school have?

DAD: And the long summer holidays … the kids are always having time off – makes them lazy.

JIMMY: *(trying to explain)* But Dad … I … er

MUM: *(coming to Jimmy's rescue)* When the boy's off school he usually has work to do. *(nudging Dad)* He works harder at school than you ever did, Bob.

JIMMY: Actually, I-I -w-w-wanted to s-s-see Grandad.

MUM: *(cross)* Bob, you've made him stutter again.

DAD: *(relenting)* Not a bad idea, Jimmy, visiting Denis. Keep the old man out of mischief.

MUM: Go on, run along with you.

JIMMY: Thanks, Mum I-I-er –

DAD: *(harsh)* And learn to construct a sentence before you speak.

JIMMY: Yes Dad … I … er … I –

DAD: *(softening)* Here, take a fiver and get yourself some lunch. Come back and tell Mum and me what your grandfather is up to.

JIMMY: *(takes the money)* Thanks Dad … I … er

(A cow moos)

DAD: The herd needs milking!

(Jimmy runs out of the house and along the road. He bumps into Gareth Endersby, a large overweight bully.)

GARETH: *(smiles)* What are you up to, Jimmy Bird?

(Jimmy does not want to reveal where he is going.)

JIMMY: *(hesitates)* I … er … I –

GARETH: *(interrupting)* And I bet your dad gave you some dosh.

JIMMY: *(lying)* No.

(Gareth lumbers over to Jimmy.)

GARETH: No? Don't give me that! If you refuse to hand over the money, I'll sneak on to your dad's farm and trample all over his courgettes. Got it?

JIMMY: N-no, you c-can't.

GARETH: *(mimics Jimmy)* N-No, you c-c-can't. *(puts his face close to Jimmy's face)* Like to bet? And what's more, I'll put all the blame on to you, sonny boy.

(Daniel Waterhouse is walking along the road. He is whistling.)

DANIEL: *(sees Jimmy)* Hi, pal. *(spots Gareth Endersby)* What are you doing, Endersby?

GARETH: *(angry)* What's it to you?

DANIEL: *(firm)* Now push off, fatboy. I know what you're up to … what you're always up to – bullying!

(Gareth waddles off)

(to Jimmy) What nasty ideas were floating through Endersby's brain this time?

JIMMY: *(hesitant)* He said … he said he'll destroy my dad's courgettes if I don't give him bribe m-money.

DANIEL: *(he wants to laugh, but he catches sight of his friend's pale face)* That boy is all bluff. If you just stood up to him, you'd be alright.

JIMMY: B-but –

DANIEL: Where are you off to? Town?

JIMMY: To see Grandad Denis.

DANIEL: Denis Chapman? What's he up to now?

JIMMY: More scientific experiments.

DANIEL: *(laughs)* He's mad is your grandad. Do you remember his time machine? Mad!

JIMMY: *(serious)* No … No … he isn't mad. Here we are!

(Jimmy knocks on his grandad's door)

GRANDAD: *(excited)* Come on in, you two. Come in, follow me. You have arrived at exactly the right moment. I am building a Continuum Nova.

JIMMY: A Continuum what?

GRANDAD: Oh, never mind. I won't bore you with the details. It's here in the annexe.

DANIEL: *(to Jimmy)* You don't stutter when you're with your grandad.

JIMMY: *(thinking)* No, no I don't.

GRANDAD: Do you see it? *(proud)* Look at that machine!

(The machine is large and metallic)

It's taken years. *(To Jimmy)* I've been working on it ever since your grandma died.

DANIEL: *(nudges Jimmy)* Is he mad?

JIMMY: *(hesitates)* No … *(emphatic)* No!

GRANDAD: This machine will take you into a parallel world. *(excited)* At last I have constructed a Continuum Nova!

DANIEL: *(to Jimmy)* He's having us on, isn't he?

JIMMY: No, I don't think he is.

GRANDAD: *(impatient)* Come on then – enter my machine. All you do is go through the machine and come back. *(sly)* When you do come back, tell me what you find. Parallel worlds can't be any worse than this one.

JIMMY: You never know, Grandad. I'm not sure I want to risk it.

GRANDAD: *(to Jimmy)* What are you, boy? A man or an amoeba?

DANIEL: *(to Jimmy)* What have we got to lose? Let's humour the old fella.

GRANDAD: *(impatient)* Come on, come on, this way!

(The boys enter the machine and a whirling noise forces them to place their hands over their ears.)

JIMMY: *(to Daniel)* It's dark in here.

DANIEL: *(shouts)* I can't hear you.

(The boys find their way out of the machine. They are back in Grandad's annexe, but it looks very different. The furniture is drab and old fashioned. Grandad has gone.)

DANIEL: *(annoyed)* What sort of joke is the old man playing on us?

JIMMY: *(puzzled)* How did Grandad change things so quickly?

(There is a crashing sound of breaking glass. Gareth Endersby enters the house, followed by two young storm troopers. Endersby is holding a gun and he is dressed as a boy of the 1940s.)

GARETH: Hands on heads, both of you.

JIMMY: *(shocked)* G-Gareth.

DANIEL: Endersby, put that gun down and stop mucking about.

GARETH: *(to the storm troopers)* Search them.

(Jimmy notices a picture on the wall. A man, resembling Adolf Hitler, stares down at them.)

JIMMY: Hitler!

(The storm troopers search Jimmy and find the five-pound note.)

GARETH: *(glances at the note)* Worthless, toy money!

(He throws the note on the floor.)

Why are you two dressed in strange clothes? And you both missed the morning youth meeting.

JIMMY: *(confused)* W-What year is this?

GARETH: Had a brain transplant, Bird? Everyone knows the year is 2002.

DANIEL: But –

GARETH: *(nasty)* But what? Stand to attention.

(A middle-aged man in Nazi uniform enters the room.)

Ah, Mr Rigby, I have detained two this morning, Sir.

RIGBY: *(brisk)* So I see, Endersby. Good boy, our glorious leader will welcome this, eh! *(to Jimmy and Daniel)* Stand to attention. Salute the portrait of our leader, Rudolph Hitler.

DANIEL: Rudolph Hitler? What sort of a game is this?

JIMMY: *(realising his grandad's machine has worked)* Actually, we shouldn't be here. This is a … er … a mistake.

DANIEL: *(realising)* You see … we were experimenting with a Continuum Nova … and …

RIGBY: *(angry)* What are you two scoundrels trying to do, eh? What are you both up to, eh? Lock them up, Endersby!

DANIEL: *(runs at Gareth and thumps him in the stomach)* Leave me alone, you bully.

(A storm trooper hits Daniel over the head with his rifle butt, and threatens Jimmy.)

JIMMY: *(panic-stricken)* N-No – d-don't – shoot.

RIGBY: *(to storm troopers)* Put these boys in the cell. We'll see how they like the cell, eh!

(Daniel is carried to the cell. Jimmy is led there by Gareth, who kicks him whenever possible. The cell is underground. It is dark and dank. At the far end of the cell is a thin, dark-haired girl. She is cowering.)

JIMMY: *(bending over his friend)* Daniel, Daniel.

DANIEL: *(coming round)* – Jim – you could have warned me – you could have told me – somebody was behind me. *(sitting up)* What a headache I've got. Your grandfather's a menace. (*sees the girl)* Hi.

JESSICA: Hello. *(she smiles at the boys)* My name's Jessica.

DANIEL: I'm Daniel, *(pointing to his friend)* he's Jimmy.

JESSICA: You don't look Jewish.

DANIEL: We're not … except, my great-grandmother was half Jewish.

JESSICA: I'm Jewish. The storm troopers usually bring Jews here before we're killed. They want to exterminate us all – but you know that!

JIMMY: *(hesitates)* N-No. No – we – we don't know that.

DANIEL: *(to Jessica)* It's a strange story – you won't believe us. We come from a different world.

JESSICA: *(laughs)* Impossible! You two are probably spies. You want to know where my sister Hannah is hiding.

DANIEL: *(to Jessica)* No. *(He feels sudden pain)* Oh, my head.

JESSICA: *(concerned)* Let me look at your wound.

JIMMY: W-Who is Rudolph Hitler?

JESSICA: *(to Daniel)* You have a nasty bruise, *(grins)* but you'll mend.

DANIEL: *(looking up at Jessica)* You have nice brown eyes.

JIMMY: *(nudges Daniel)* Can't you leave any girl alone? *(to Jessica)* Who is Rudolph Hitler?

JESSICA: You have heard of Adolf Hitler?

DANIEL/JIMMY: Yes.

JESSICA: Rudolph is Adolf's son. After the fall of Britain –

DANIEL: Fall of Britain? We won the war in 1945.

JESSICA: Sadly, no. Our history books tell us Adolf's scientists invented a nuclear bomb that destroyed most of America – in – what was the year, 1944. After the fall of Britain, in 1948, Hitler married Eva Braun. He died soon afterwards. The Reich was ruled by a coalition until Rudolph took power in 1988, aged forty. *(tearful)* I was born in hiding – there are so few Jews left. But this evil regime will not destroy us, we cannot all be wiped out. A remnant will survive!

DANIEL: *(softly)* Jessica – we will help you escape.

JIMMY: *(surprised)* We will?

DANIEL: *(to Jimmy)* This is still your grandfather's house. You must know every inch of the place.

JIMMY: *(thinking)* Yes – we are in the old part of the house, in what should be a storage room. *(brightens)* Under the floorboards are some steps and a passage.

DANIEL: Well, let's start looking!

(They find a rotten plank and pull at the floorboards.)

JESSICA: Here we are … steps.

DANIEL: Let's pull some of the boards up and sneak through.

(searches his coat pocket) Ah, a torch, that's lucky! Let's go!

(The threesome squeeze down the steps.)

Where does this passage lead to, Jimmy?

JIMMY: The wine cellar! Follow me.

(The threesome find themselves in a dark passageway that leads into an empty cellar.)

DANIEL: Where now, Jimmy?

JIMMY: This door should lead to the woods at the back of the house.

GARETH: Not so fast! Hands on heads!

(Gareth has a gun in his hands.)

DANIEL: Going to shoot us, Endersby?

GARETH: *(laughing)* That is the general idea, yes!

(He raises his gun)

DANIEL: But you can' t shoot us all at once. Who will you choose first?

(Daniel walks towards Gareth)

And what will Rigby say, if you have shot a boy, an old school mate?

GARETH: *(matter of fact)* Prisoners helping a Jew to escape – had no choice but to kill.

(Daniel kicks Gareth in the shins, grabs his gun and lands a blow in Endersby's ample guts.)

DANIEL: *(to Jimmy)* That's the way to deal with cowards, Jimmy. Come on, show us the way into the wild woods. At least we have a gun.

(They run across the yard, over a fence and into the woods.)

SCENE TWO

The three children are crouching at the edge of the woods. There are steam trains running slowly along railway tracks.

JIMMY: Things haven't moved along, technologically.

JESSICA: They have stagnated!

DANIEL: In our world, there are trains that run without steam, most people own fast cars. And – your people have their own country, Israel.

JESSICA: *(smiling)* Hopefully, this will all happen in my world, in this evil world – one day.

JIMMY: Evil does not survive for ever.

JESSICA: This evil has spread across the world, since the 1930s.

DANIEL: *(practical)* What do we do, Jessica?

JESSICA: We jump a train, and that will take us to Peterborough, which is the central terminus – almost every train will end up there. I must try to find my sister, Hannah. We'll jump the next train just as it gathers steam.

JIMMY: *(afraid)* We will?

DANIEL: *(determined)* We will, amoeba. *(to Jessica)* I shall leave the gun under this oak tree.

JESSICA: *(smiling)* Hold my hand, Jimmy. We'll jump on the train together.

DANIEL: *(teasing)* I'm scared, too!

(The train chugs close to the children.)

JESSICA: Right, now!

(They jump on to the train as it gathers speed.)

You boys are risking your lives for me. Without identity cards nobody can travel.

DANIEL: Well, this is quite an adventure.

JIMMY: *(quickly)* An adventure I could do without. *(afraid)* Shouldn't we go back? Back to the Continuum Nova? Shouldn't we get back to Grandad?

DANIEL: Come on mouse, we need to find Hannah.

JIMMY: *(grumpy)* Just 'cause you fancy Jessica.

(They move into a carriage and sit down. A ticket inspector arrives.)

INSPECTOR: Tickets, please!

JIMMY: Actually, we didn't have time to buy the tickets.

DANIEL: *(thinking quickly)* We were in a hurry.

INSPECTOR: *(sharp)* Identity cards?

JIMMY: *(tearful)* To tell you the truth … er … we l-left them a-at home.

DANIEL: We left home in a hurry.

INSPECTOR: *(laughs)* Ha, ha! Out for a free ride to Peterborough are we? Did just the same thing when I was your age. Cheeky young fella, I was! But that was a long time ago. Sixty I am – ten more years and I'll be retired, if old Rudolph'll let me.

JIMMY: *(sweating)* Y-Yes.

INSPECTOR: Well now, you three young 'uns don't seem like menaces to the state to me. *(laughs)* Make sure you're back home in time for tea.

(He moves off.)

JIMMY: Phew!

JESSICA: *(relieved)* You two were great. If he'd realised who I was, it would have been the death penalty for refusing to wear the star of David on my clothes.

DANIEL: *(thinking)* How long does it take to reach Peterborough?

JESSICA: About an hour.

(An old man shuffles up to them. He is the only other person in the carriage.)

GEORGE: *(whispers)* I couldn't help but overhear you.

JESSICA: *(afraid)* Oh, spare the boys. They are not from here, they live in a different … er … place.

GEORGE: *(whispers hoarsely)* If you alight from the train at Peterborough, you will never return.

JIMMY: *(afraid)* W-Why?

GEORGE: The Inspector knows who you are. … wireless confirmation. He looks pleasant ... but trust nobody.

(The old man shuffles back to his seat.)

DANIEL: *(whispers)* How do we know we can trust the old man?

JESSICA: *(firmly)* I know! It is providence he was here, on this train.

DANIEL: You know him?

JESSICA: *(smiling)* I know of him … a war hero, before the defeat. He led the resistance movement most of his life. George Pascoe is his name.

JIMMY: *(fearful)* Th-This is scary. I-I need to occupy myself. We need to do something, to pass the time.

JESSICA: Tell me about your world. What do you like doing?

JIMMY: Watching television –

JESSICA: *(confused)* What a vision?

DANIEL: *(enthusiastic)* And playing games on the computer, surfing the net, playing CDs–

JESSICA: What are you talking about? You inhabit a strange world.

DANIEL: We'll explain, that'll help pass the time away.

(An hour later, the train stops at red lights, outside Peterborough railway station.)

JESSICA: *(urgent)* Follow me – we must jump off the train, just as the lights turn green.

JIMMY: *(afraid)* I-I don't like h-heights.

DANIEL: *(teasing)* Come on mighty mouse, jump or die.

(The three desperados jump off the train. They hear a voice urgently calling them.

HERMAN: *(shouting)* Quickly, over here.

(There is the sound of gunfire.)

JESSICA: *(surprised)* Herman! *(to the boys)* His father was from Germany, but he is on our side.

HERMAN: The uprising is planned for tonight. The partisans are behind us, in the woods.

HANNAH: *(rushing up to embrace Jessica)* Jessica, are you alright, are you safe? Providence has reunited us!

JESSICA: *(overjoyed)* Hannah!

(They hug each other)

HERMAN: There are about thirty of us. We should take the station, but there are hundreds of partisans attacking throughout the country.

BERNARD: *(emerging, grinning)* Then Britain will be free of the Nazi scourge. Free forever!

(People cheer Bernard)

HANNAH: Yes, Bernard – you are right.

JIMMY: *(to Daniel)* This is where we split, get back to our world, Grandad – right?

DANIEL: *(teasing)* Oh mighty man of courage – *(serious)* No, you are right!

HERMAN: The one I want to catch is Rigby. He killed my brother.

JESSICA: *(excited)* I know where he is – we just left him.

HERMAN: Take me to him!

JESSICA: *(to the boys)* This will mean jumping another train.

JIMMY: *(determined)* I'll do anything to get back to my world.

(A few hours later, the partisans are back at Jimmy's grandfather's house.)

HERMAN: Let me find and destroy Rigby!

(Rigby and Gareth Endersby are together, talking in loud whispers.)

RIGBY: You're a coward, Endersby.

GARETH: Yes sir, sorry sir!

HERMAN: *(stepping from the shadows)* Turn Rigby, hell hound.

RIGBY: *(draws a gun)* What is the meaning of this?

BERNARD: *(with gun)* Drop your weapons, or face instant death.

(Rigby and Gareth drop their guns.)

BERNARD: You two are my prisoners.

JIMMY: C-come on, Daniel, let's find the Continuum Nova, let's get back to Grandad.

DANIEL: Good idea – *(to Jessica)* come back with us, Jessica. Our world is better than this. You can see my computer!

JESSICA: *(looks at Hannah and hesitates)* I can't … I can't!

JIMMY: *(to Jessica)* Bring Hannah too – even for a short while.

JESSICA: Well, perhaps …

DANIEL: Have a quick peek at our world. I bet you've never heard of micro-chips or e-mail, have you?

JIMMY: Or lasers, or lap-tops or videos –

HANNAH: *(excited)* Show us the way into your world.

(They make their way into the outhouse, which has pictures of Rudolph Hitler displayed.)

JIMMY: Come on – f -follow me.

DANIEL: *(interested)* Do you realise, with all the excitement, you have almost lost your stutter, Jimmy Giant Mouse?

JIMMY: *(ignoring Daniel)* Here we are – the Continuum Nova.

(Jimmy goes into the machine.)

DANIEL: Come on Jessica – explore my world.

JESSICA: *(nervous)* Daniel – I, I'm afraid!

DANIEL: *(laughs)* You, afraid? You, who are under threat of death here!

JESSICA: My world is what I am used to – yours is unknown.

DANIEL: *(firmly)* Hold my hand and I shall take you to my world.

(She places her hand in his.)

Here goes!

(As the machine works, Daniel notices Jessica becomes more ghost-like, less substantial.)

Jessica!

JESSICA: *(faint)* I can't – can't enter your world. I am fading – becoming nothing. *(She lets go of Daniel's hand)* Goodbye Daniel.

DANIEL: *(desperate)* Jessica!

ACT TWO
SCENE ONE

The boys are back in Grandad's house. Everything looks just as it did when the boys left.

JIMMY: *(relieved)* Back at last. *(shouts)* Grandad?

DANIEL: Did that parallel world really exist? Jessica just faded away.

JIMMY: *(shouts)* Grandad?

DANIEL: Suppose we've just entered another possible world, where the Russians invaded and the Communists beat the free West in the 1980s?

JIMMY: *(scared)* Don't frighten me, Daniel.

DANIEL: Come on, brave heart, let's find your grandad.

JIMMY: *(becoming anxious)* He m-might be in his g-garden round the back, near the wood.

(They open the back door. The woods are bare, as if all the trees are dying.)

DANIEL: *(trying to joke)* It looks as if acid rain has done its trick here.

JIMMY: Look at those silvery streaks everywhere. Like giant slug trails.

DANIEL: I don't like this – back inside the house.

(Inside Grandad's room, there are two slug-like creatures with leathery hands and short brown arms.)

SLUG 1: *(spoken in a robotic voice)* Stay, aliens.

SLUG 2: Move and you die.

DANIEL: *(to Jimmy)* Do as he says, he appears pretty sure that moving will mean death.

JIMMY: *(afraid)* N-No need to c-convince m-me, D-Daniel.

SLUG 1: *(to Slug 2)* They will work in the mines. Take them to the transporter. Put them to sleep first.

SLUG 2: Yes, sir.

(The boys wake up in the underground mines. Jessica is standing over them.)

DANIEL: Jessica? Is this a dream?

JESSICA: *(confused)* How do you know who I am?

DANIEL: Never mind – it's a long story.

JIMMY: W-we're captured.

DANIEL: Yes Jimmy, you have the whole picture. *(to Jessica)* We come from far away. What's happened here? Who are these ugly slug creatures?

JESSICA: *(very surprised)* Don't you know? Don't they control the whole Earth?

DANIEL: Not quite – at least, not all possible Earths.

JESSICA: *(explaining)* The ugly creatures are called Slargs. Their own planet was virtually destroyed by their mining activities. They need a substance deep within the earth to survive. They eat coal. When coal runs out, they will die.

DANIEL: So – we are sent to mine coal.

JESSICA: Yes, and when the coal runs out, it is believed that they will destroy the planet and invade another planet. These creatures will destroy the universe.

GARETH: *(appears with a whip)*
Keep working,
or I'll flog you!

JESSICA: *(whispers)* Gareth Endersby …
he works for the Slargs.

GARETH: *(raises his whip)* Keep working, girl – or you'll get this across your back.

*(He cracks the whip.
Jessica shrinks away.)*

JESSICA: *(to Daniel)* He beats us, I have bruises across my shoulders.

(Gareth lashes his whip down on Jessica's slim back.)

JESSICA: *(cries out in pain)* Ahhhh!

DANIEL: *(stands up)* Beat a woman, would you Endersby?

GARETH: How dare the slave talk!

(Gareth raises his whip again, but Daniel grabs the handle and punches Endersby in the guts. The bully doubles up.)

DANIEL: *(to Jessica and Jimmy)* Come on, we've got to escape this dreadful place.

JIMMY: W-What about the Slargs?

JESSICA: Out there, in the countryside, there is a freedom group.

DANIEL: Your sister, Hannah, is she part of the group?

JESSICA: *(shocked)* How did you know? Who are you?

DANIEL: *(smiling)* Never mind, I'll tell you when I can!

RIGBY: *(with gun)* Hold it, slaves!

(Daniel, Jimmy and Jessica stop in their tracks)

JIMMY: R-Rigby!

DANIEL: I forgot about Rigby.

RIGBY: Mr Rigby to you lot.

(Behind the group is old George. He also carries a gun.)

GEORGE: *(quietly)* Drop your weapon, Rigby – or I'll blow out your brains.

JIMMY: Good old George, he's saved us twice now.

GEORGE: Go to the top of the mine. The resistance fighters plan to attack tonight. Take care!

(The threesome reach the top of the mine shaft.)

HERMAN: Halt, who goes there?

JESSICA: Three volunteers for the freedom movement.

HANNAH: *(surprised)* Jessica, I recognise your voice.

JESSICA: *(delighted)* Hannah!

(They embrace)

BERNARD: *(urgent)* Come on, no time to waste. *(to Daniel)* The Slargs die if they come into contact with salt. We've secretly mined tons of the stuff. We're ready to attack, with salt – but there are dangers.

JESSICA: *(excited)* Perhaps we can free our planet of the Slarg scourge.

JIMMY: *(to Daniel)* Time to split!

(Daniel nods)

Back to the Continuum Nova!

DANIEL: You wait until I see your grandfather. *(angry)* We could have been killed, twice!

(The boys make their way back to Grandad's house – the mines were just the other side of the dying wood.)

JIMMY: We want either a better world, or our own world.

(They enter the Continuum Nova.)

DANIEL: Let's hope we find our own world.

SCENE TWO

The boys enter Grandad's room once more.

GRANDAD: *(excited)* Ah, what did you think of the machine, boys? Splendid, wasn't it?

JIMMY: Well –w-we're back!

GRANDAD: *(excited)* Well?

DANIEL: I think you'd better take a look at the parallel worlds yourself, Mr Chapman.

GRANDAD: *(excited)* Oh, yes, I will.

JIMMY: I-it's dangerous, Grandad.

GRANDAD: *(impatient)* Oh yes, yes – every adventure is dangerous. Isn't that the point about adventures?

DANIEL: Yes, I suppose so!

GRANDAD: Well, I won't detain you any longer. I promised the new landlord of 'The Sporting Chance' that I'd take part in the pub bowling competition. Mr Rigby would be disappointed if I let him down.

JIMMY: Rigby?

GRANDAD: Yes, a nice, quiet sort of fellow.

JIMMY: *(anxious)* Don't trust Rigby!

GRANDAD: *(alarmed)* Why ever not? He appears to be a gentleman whom I could trust.

DANIEL: Erm – he doesn't react to adverse circumstances particularly well.

JIMMY: *(to Daniel)* N-nicely put, D-Daniel.

GRANDAD: *(surprised)* Really? Anyhow, if I give you some money for entering my machine, you can buy yourselves some sweets. You could try the new shop.

DANIEL: The one in the high street, past the greengrocer's?

GRANDAD: That's the one. You'd like the girl who works there – nice girl – the name of Jessica, Jessica Cohen.

DANIEL: *(urgent)* I've got to see her … I must go!

(Daniel dashes off)

GRANDAD: *(confused)* Now where's that young Daniel run off to? A funny boy, dashing off before I've given him any cash!

JIMMY: *(laughing)* I think he wants to meet Jessica Cohen. He met her …somewhere else.

(Grandad nods and smiles to himself.)

JIMMY: Well, Grandad, I'd better get back home. Dad might want some of my help.

(As Jimmy leaves he takes one last look at his grandad – whose eyes appear a strange orange colour.)

(to himself) Funny – have Grandad's eyes changed, or was it a trick of the light?

(Jimmy is whistling to himself as he walks home.)

GARETH: What are you up to, Jimmy Bird?

JIMMY: I-I've been to see my g-grandad.

GARETH: And I bet he gave you some dosh?

JIMMY: Perhaps.

GARETH: And what's that supposed to mean, Bird-brain? Give me some dosh or I'll destroy all your dad's lovely runner beans! Got it?

JIMMY: N-No. You c-can't.

GARETH: And what's more, I'll put all the blame on to you, sonny boy. Especially now your mate Daniel isn't here to protect you.

JIMMY: *(finding new courage)* Then I'll p-protect myself!

(He punches Gareth in his ample guts. Gareth doubles up.)

JIMMY: Am I a man or an amoeba? A man! All bullies are cowards!

(He runs home, pleased with himself.)

DAD: Glad to see you, Jimmy. You're just in time to help me pick the peas.

JIMMY: Great! It's good to be back in my world.

(He turns to look at his dad, whose eyes appear to flash and glow orange.)

(confused) Dad? *(pause)* Am I back in my own world?

MIRROR WORLD.

ACTIVITIES
ACT ONE: SCENE ONE

Discussion
Do you feel that Dad is too harsh on Jimmy?
What are the outward signs that Jimmy lacks confidence?
What evidence have we already got that Gareth is a bully and that Daniel is more confident than Jimmy?
Is there evidence that Grandad also treats Jimmy as a coward?

Chat Show
In groups, imagine that you have the chance to interview some of the characters on a television chat show. Write down a number of questions that you would like to ask each character. Take it in turns to ask questions and then answer the questions in role.
The characters invited onto the chat show are: Denis Chapman (Grandad), Gareth Endersby, Rigby, Daniel and Jimmy.

Research
In many ways, this play is not so much about a parallel world, but the real world of Adolf Hitler's Nazi Germany (1933 - 1945). Using the library, C.D. Roms and the internet, find out about World War Two (1939-1945) and about how the Nazis treated the Jews. Here are some books you might like to read:

'The Diary Of Anne Frank' by Anne Frank
'A Candle in the Dark' by Adele Geras
'No Hiding Place' by Corrie Ten Boom.

Writing
Imagine you are Jessica. Write a diary featuring your escape from the Nazis and describing how you met Daniel and Jimmy.

Who are the victims in the play? List names of people in the play that you feel are victims in some way. You could set out your ideas like this:

Victims	**Why?**
Jimmy	Bullied by Gareth Endersby

ACT ONE: SCENE TWO

Discussion
Grandad has placed the children in danger by allowing them to enter a parallel world. Do you think he realised this? Is he a responsible or an irresponsible person? Relay your answer to another group and see what they think.

Weakest link
If you were in a dangerous situation with the characters in the play, which of them do you think might let you down? Have a class vote to remove the weakest link. Think about all the virtues and weaknesses of each character before you vote.

Freeze-framing
Imagine you are the three children jumping on the train. Freeze-frame the moment you are about to jump. Who is afraid, who has experience of train-jumping and who is finding the danger exciting? How can you convey how each one is feeling inside? Think about body movement and expressions.

Improvisation
Old George is on a dangerous mission. Imagine George and a group of patriots are discussing tactics to rid themselves of the Nazis. Improvise the discussion and talk about the mission. Is it a success? Does George escape or die?

Jessica has to return to her sister and tell her that she was unable to enter Daniel's world. Write a short dialogue between her and her sister. They might talk about Jessica's disappointment and about their hopes and plans for the future.

GENERAL

Discussion

Looking at the play as a whole, who do you think is the nastiest character in the play? Rigby or Endersby? Use evidence from the text to back up your answers.

Reread the play. What are the themes in the play? List all the possible themes, pass to another group, and see if your lists coincide.

Mime

In small groups, mime a short scene from the play. Finally, all groups can act out their mimes and the class can vote on the best group mime.

Writing

Look at some of the characters. What do you feel about them all now that you have read the whole play?

Characters	**Main Points**
Grandad	Irresponsible
Jimmy	
Daniel	
Gareth	
Jessica	
George	
Herman	

Imagine Jimmy is not back in his own world. Remember, he thought his grandad had orange eyes when he returned home. Write another adventure story entitled 'The Land of Orange Eyes.' What will happen in this alternative world and how will Jimmy and friends escape?